OUR
STORY
MAGIC

GCINA MHLOPHE

UNIVERSITY OF KwaZulu-Natal Press

Published in 2006 by University of KwaZulu-Natal Press
Private Bag X01
Scottsville, 3209
South Africa
Email: books@ukzn.ac.za
Website: www.ukznpress.co.za

ISBN 10: 1-86914-111-3
ISBN 13: 978-1-86914-111-0

Editors: Lesley Beake and Andrea Nattrass
Layout and design: Flying Ant Designs
Cover design: Flying Ant Designs
Cover illustrations: Jeannie Kinsler, Lalelani Mbhele and Kalle Becker

Printed and bound by Interpak Books, Pietermaritzburg

I dedicate this book to my family, my husband and our beautiful
daughter Nomakhwezi – thanks for all your love and support.
And to the many parents and grandparents in South Africa who strive
to bring joy and warmth to their little ones even in the worst of times,
keeping hope alive, often performing little miracles each day.

AUTHOR'S NOTE

There was a time, not so long ago, when I really believed in magic. You see, my world was an enchanted one with all the stories I listened to almost every day. My Gogo told me stories in which animals and people alike performed magic again and again. So why not in my life?

Why could I not split myself into two when I did not feel like going to school? One me could go and learn and the other me could stay at home and play! Why could I not find a clever little bird that could clean our whole house on a Saturday morning or at least wash my school uniform and polish my shoes? Surely that was not too much to ask?

Well, slowly but surely it dawned on me that the story world was very different from the real world in which I lived – a world filled with ordinary people and animals.

But then again, when I look back over the years, I can see that I was always surrounded with a kind of magic. Every day parents performed little miracles. They provided for us and sacrificed all kinds of pleasures in order to give us that little bit of magic. A mother did not eat something tasty, saving it for her children. Parents saved money, little by little, in order to buy a much-needed pair of shoes . . . or pay for an all important school trip. I clearly remember total strangers opening their hearts to help a person just when it looked like all was lost. In this way, our parents and grandparents taught us that there was always hope. Even if it took a miracle, we could come out of a very difficult time in our lives.

Today we still see many miracles, even ones that remind us of the characters in these stories such as the brave ox Bhatom or the snake prince Mamba kaMaqhuba. How exciting it is to see ambitious little creatures such as the tortoise who wanted to be queen; she makes us look at what dreams we also have in life. What heights we wish to reach. But we know too that we must take care and listen to good advice.

Please enjoy *Our Story Magic* and never stop believing that you could also possess some magic powers now and again. Your heart knows it. My heart knows it. Magic is still in the here and now.

CONTENTS

SUN and the MOON

Illustrations by Jeannie Kinsler

THERE WAS A TIME, long, long ago, when the world was very young and life was totally different to what we now know it to be. The days were long. The nights were short. The Sun and the Moon were married.

They lived in a beautiful house in the middle of Africa. What strong love they had for one another. You could see it in their faces. The Moon was round, serene and her face was radiant with love. Her gentle voice was so reassuring to her loved ones.

The Sun was very warm and charming and he had such an adventurous spirit. He loved exploring the world he lived in. Then he would return to tell his wife and children about all that he had seen.

Their children were very beautiful indeed; they used to shine and sparkle as they felt the love of their mother, the Moon, and their father, the Sun. There were so *many* children – and they almost all looked the same! It was so hard to think up a different name for each and every one of them that Sun and Moon simply decided to call them . . . Stars. They gave them all the same name because they loved them all the same way and those children knew very well how loved they were.

From time to time Sun would leave home in the morning and set off on an adventure to explore places he had never seen before. He hopped over hills and mountains, observing and wondering, and then came home to his wife and children to tell them all that he had seen. Next time he might float over the forests, over long and vast stretches of land as the grass seemed to sway gently in the wind, calling to him to come and dance a little. Every afternoon when he returned to his family, the children sat and listened to their father's stories and they tried to imagine the places he told them about. The Moon just listened and smiled quietly. How beautiful she looked!

One morning the Sun went away on his adventures again, promising to return with more stories. This time he went further than he had ever gone before. He just kept going and his heart was beating really fast with excitement.

He was hoping to see more than the usual. He wanted something different. He kept going until he saw something shining in the distance and he hurried to find out what it was.

What a shock he got! There was something – or someone – who was shimmering and dancing in his light. Stretching out as far as his eyes could see . . . was water, water and more water.

The Sun stood there, staring in amazement. 'Who are you? How come I have never seen you before?' he asked.

'Whooooosh, whaaaaaa! Whoooosh, whaaaaaa!' she whispered. 'You may not know who I am but I know who *you* are and I have seen you travelling all over the land.'

She smiled. 'Whooooosh, whaaaaaa! Whoooosh, whaaaaaa!' The Sun was

quite captivated. On and on she went, shimmering and dancing in her own rhythm.

'But I don't know *you*! Please tell me who you are!' pleaded the Sun in complete amazement.

'I am the Sea, and I have been here since the beginning of time. I don't know what you mean when you say you have never seen me before,' she replied, smiling and moving her large body in her unique way.

And then she showed him her many, many children who all lived in her body – the dolphins, the sharks, turtles, and many others. They peeped at the Sun and went back into the Sea's body, some of them smiling shyly, others commenting how very warm the Sun's rays were.

Later that day the Sun went back home to tell his wife about all that he had seen. The children were mesmerised. They wished to see what he was telling them about. They were so curious, but the Moon listened to the excited telling – the happy way Sun described the Sea – and she hardly made a comment. Only 'Uhmmm' (very quietly to herself).

The next time the Sun went to visit the Sea they talked about his extremely beautiful wife and children.

'I *wish* you could meet them all; they are so very special,' Sun said.

'That would be wonderful. Maybe I will meet them one day,' replied the Sea.

'Hey! Wait a minute! I have an idea. Why don't you come and visit us tomorrow?' asked the Sun excitedly.

'I would love to, but how big is your house? As you can see, I am a fairly large woman,' the Sea replied.

'Well – now that you mention it – our house is not very big really. I will have to do something about that. I will come and tell you when we have enlarged our house, then you and your children are all welcome to visit,' said the Sun, and he rushed off back home.

He told his family that he had invited the Sea to come and visit them. There was so much work to be done, breaking and rebuilding the house to make it extra large – more than double its original size. And the walls had to be much higher too, said the Sun, to hold all of the Sea's many children.

Once they had finished the house then they got to the food preparation, cooking many pots full of every kind of food imaginable. When everything was ready, the Sun rushed off to call the Sea. He was so excited for her to meet his lovely wife and children.

'Hey, Sea! The time is here! We are ready for you. Come on over!' he called happily.

The Sea had been waiting and she wasted no time. She whoooooshed and whaaaaaaed over the hills and over the mountains, following the Sun further and further inland. The journey continued until the Sun arrived at home and called excitedly to his family: 'Look . . . over there! Sea is coming closer!'

And yes, indeed, they could see the Sea from a long way off, whooshing closer at great speed. Over the forests, 'Whooooosh!' Over the valleys, 'Whooooosh!' Faster and faster. Water and more water everywhere. She was getting closer.

She was almost at the front door when the Moon looked up and saw that, even though the Sea had begun to arrive, the rest of her was still over there, as far as the Moon's eyes could see!

Oh, the land was completely covered in the Sea's water. Moon nervously whispered to her husband, 'Don't you think she is a bit too large even for our new house? Maybe it is better to give her the food from here and right now.'

But the Sun pushed his wife aside, a little embarrassed by what she was suggesting. He smiled at the Sea. 'Meet my wife, Moon, and please do come inside. The food is all ready for you.'

There was hardly a greeting from the Sea. She just rushed into the house with all her hungry children and started eating. They moved so fast and so greedily. The Sea's children did not care to meet the Stars.

The Sea kept swelling and swelling in the house and all that salty water spoilt the taste of the carefully prepared meals. Soon there was no space for the Sun, the Moon *or* their children, the Stars – and still the Sea was not yet all there. More water was coming.

Finally the walls could not take it any longer; they burst and fell apart. 'Hayi! To think I told him! Hayi!' grumbled the Moon under her breath.

This was it! She had had enough. She turned to her children and said, 'Come with me. We are *going*!'

They set off, higher and higher up into the sky. The children were fascinated by the vast open space called the sky.

'Oh Mama, we love this place, why have we not come here before?' they cried.

'I have a feeling this is really where we belong,' she replied, forcing a smile.

'But when is our father, the Sun, coming?' the Stars asked.

'Mpf! Don't talk to me about *that* one!' replied their mother, still very angry with her husband.

The children were not sure if they understood everything, but this new place was such fun! They moved from one part of the sky to the next, exploring just as the Sun had done before.

Back home the Sun was so sorry for what had happened and he was also angry with himself. He had not meant to chase away his beloved wife. He tried to follow her, thinking of nice, kind words he would use to let her know just how much he still loved her and the children. But his mind was all confused.

He wanted his family to understand too that the Sea's visit was only to share with them some of the adventures he had enjoyed. Oh, it was all too difficult for him to think clearly. He sat down to rest for a while and fell into a deep, troubled sleep.

His family roamed the sky until they too were tired and fell asleep. When the Sun woke up he went looking for them. But he could not find them. He had composed a beautiful poem and he was shining brighter and hotter with love.

But no matter how fast he moved in the sky, he could not find them.

When he finally fell asleep again, Moon and the Stars woke up and travelled all over the world, having new adventures every day. They even saw the Sea going back to her home at the Ocean and leaving some of her water children in new rivers and lakes.

So it was that the Sun moved in the day and Moon and her children, the Stars, moved at night. For many weeks, months, and years they missed each other. But Sun and Moon's love for one another was too strong to die; they longed for each other every day.

And from time to time they steal a few moments to be together in a tight and hot embrace. People call it an eclipse, but it is the rare chance that Sun and Moon have to be together. They throw a dark cloak over the world because they don't want any humans watching.

Cosi, cosi, iyaphela

HERE I REST MY STORY

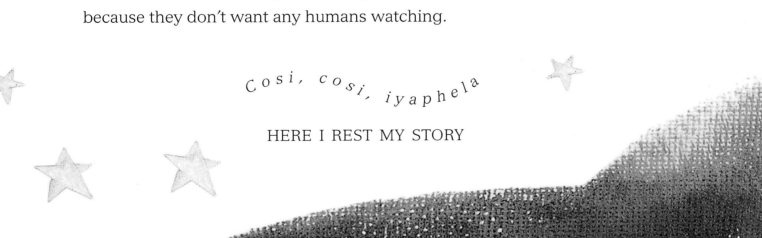

BRAVE OX BHATOM

Illustrations by Lalelani Mbhele

Kwesukesukela
Chosi

It happened a long time ago
We are ready to listen

IT IS SAID that there was a family with a large herd of cattle. The cattle were admired by many of the neighbours in their village. The family's only son Dumile was a very good herd boy. He took pride in the way he cared for his father's cattle.

Dumile and his friends also played wonderful games while they were out in the hills and plains with the cattle. At the end of each day the boys brought the cattle back home after a last drink at the river. Dumile counted the cattle to make sure that none had gone missing and, in this, he was helped by his favourite ox, Bhatom.

This ox seemed to understand him very well. When he whistled for Bhatom to lead the other cattle home, the ox did this with joy. His strong neck and head held high, he ran down the hill with the rest of his herd following happily.

Dumile would raise his voice and proudly praise him:

Bahole nkomo kababa
Bhatom nkabi empondo zimhlophe okweqhwa
Nkabi emandla esantshwa nayizinkunzi ezaziwayo
Wena okuhlakanipha buxaka osiyazi
Sihlobo nomsizi wami woqobo!

Lead them ox of my father
Bhatom, ox with the snow-white horns
Ox so strong the fiercest bulls fear you
You whose intelligence confuses wise men
My very true friend and helper!

In the evenings when the first star appeared in the western sky, grandparents told the children story after story as the families gathered around the fire. Dumile loved this time most – the magic spells that saved the heroes in many of the stories. He could just see it all in his mind's eye. He even dreamed of travelling to those fantastic places when he fell asleep.

The years were good. The rains came on time and people had great harvests from their fields, so they were really happy.

* * *

One day Dumile was up in the hills with other herd boys. The sky was a bright blue and there was not a single cloud in sight. There was a gentle breeze blowing, but the winter sun was warm on their skins as the boys enjoyed a lazy afternoon telling jokes and laughing quietly.

Then the cattle started to move around nervously and pushed each other this way and that. Some bellowed loudly. The boys immediately jumped up and took their sticks, their eyes searching for the danger that had unsettled the animals.

And indeed there *was* great danger. A group of about ten huge, man-eating ogres was coming towards them. One of them was enough to scare any man or child. But now there were so many of them!

Some of the boys turned and ran for their lives. Others quickly tried to drive their cattle to safety. The animals were terrified and confused. Only Bhatom stood proudly and looked at the approaching ogres without a trace of fear.

Dumile tried to call to his brave ox to lead their cattle to safety. Bhatom did not move. The whole of Dumile's herd of cattle waited for their leader to show them the way. When he did not move they all stood there nervously looking at him.

The man-eating ogres were watching all that was going on. They decided that this unusually large and brave ox was just what they were looking for.

'Young man, we will take this ox with us. Is it your father's?' one of the ugly ogres asked.

'Yes it is my father's,' Dumile answered, hardly able to speak with fear.

The ogres kicked the ox to move. Bhatom stood there and stared at them with fearless eyes. Again and again they hit him with their large sticks, but the ox would not move. The ugly ogres had never seen anything like this in their lives.

'What is this? Has your ox grown roots from fear?' they demanded.

'Bhatom does not know what fear is,' answered Dumile quietly.

'Then we will teach him! We shall take you with us and you will make him come along. Or both of you are dead meat right here and now!' the ogres growled.

The boy stood close to his beloved ox friend and sang a song that went like this:

Hamba nabo, Bhatom
We nkomo kababa, Bhatom
Singafa sonke, Bhatom
Bhatom, sobuya Bhatom!

Go with them, Bhatom
Ox of my father, Bhatom
We'll all be killed, Bhatom
Bhatom, but we'll be back, Bhatom!

Bhatom looked at his friend Dumile, threw his head back and bellowed out loud. Then he began to move, with the ugly ogres cheering and showing their dirty teeth as they drove him away.

Dumile asked one of his friends to take his herd back home; he would go wherever the ogres took him and Bhatom.

For hours they walked, on and on, to a strange place where Dumile had never been before. He was terrified but he tried not to show it. Having

Bhatom there with him also gave him some courage. When they got to a big river the brave ox drank some water and then sat down and refused to move any further. The ogres tried to make him cross the river but Bhatom seemed to have turned into a rock that could not be moved. The ogres were furious!

'Tell your ox to go, or we will kill and eat you both right here and now!' said one of the ogres who looked as if he was their leader. He was tired of all this nonsense.

Dumile sang his song once more:

Wela lo mfula, Bhatom
We nkomo kababa, Bhatom
Singafa sonke, Bhatom
Bhatom, sobuya Bhatom!

Cross this river, Bhatom
Ox of my father, Bhatom
We'll all be killed, Bhatom
Bhatom, but we'll be back, Bhatom

Hearing this song the brave ox stood up and crossed the river easily, with Dumile riding on his back. The water was high but the ogres were so very big it was easy for them to walk across.

At long last they reached the home of the man-eating ogres. An old woman ogre was sitting by the fire with huge pots full of boiling water, waiting for the meat to arrive.

The ogres took their sharpest spears and threw them at Bhatom. But every single one of them simply touched his skin and bent before it fell down to the ground. Again and again they tried and the spears fell to the ground. The leader took his own spear, went straight for the neck and stabbed with all his might, but the spear broke into two and he hurt his own hand.

'Hey you! Sing your foolish song and let this bull be killed! Do you hear me!' he bellowed, and his booming voice echoed across the hills and mountains.

With a shaking voice Dumile sang his song, begging his ox to die.

The next spear killed him and all the ogres clapped their hands and shouted happily. Dumile could not bear to look as they cut Bhatom to pieces and filled the pots with his meat.

He sat next to a big rock and cried. His heart was broken. What now? Were they going to kill him and eat him too?

But the ogres were only interested in his ox that seemed to have magic powers. They focused on the boiling pots and got ready to eat. They even forgot about the boy being there. They were singing loudly, a song that sounded more like noise. It was even uglier than all their ugly faces put together! Dumile put his fingers in his ears and cried some more.

It was not long before the ogres took the pots off the fire and put the meat on large wooden trays. Their mouths were watering and they ate the meat hot as it was. They pushed the old woman who had been tending the fire aside and did not give her even a little piece. When they were done, they threw the bones at Dumile, hurting him each time, and told him they would eat him later.

Dumile was in great pain after he had been hurt so many times. He knew now that he would be eaten next. The ogres fell asleep one after the other next to the dying fire. The old woman sat quietly and dozed off too.

Soon there was only the sound of the ogres' loud snoring that filled the air. Up in the sky there was a little slice of a new moon and the stars were growing into thousands of sad eyes watching the boy.

Dumile stood up slowly. He collected all the bones of his beloved friend Bhatom and put them into the skin that lay near the place where the ogres had killed the ox. He took his stick and began to sing, very quietly beating a rhythm on the bundle of skin and bones:

Vuka sambe, Bhatom
We nkomo kababa, Bhatom

Singafa sonke, Bhatom
Bhatom, sobuya Bhatom!

Wake up let's go, Bhatom
Ox of my father, Bhatom
We'll all be killed, Bhatom
Bhatom, but we'll be back, Bhatom!

And wake up he did!

What a magical sight it was, first to see the bones move inside the skin. Then the horns to emerge on his head and his eyes wide open. His powerful shoulders were next and then the rest of the body standing proudly on all four legs!

As each part of the body came alive, the ogre who had eaten it simply collapsed and died right there and then. Their stomachs ripped open.

The old woman sat and watched everything that was happening. Her old, grey eyes had never seen anything like this. She was speechless as she saw Dumile climb onto the brave ox's back and gallop away.

They travelled all night long, heading back home. Bhatom knew exactly where to go. Dumile was extremely tired but he was also overwhelmed by all that had happened on that day and night.

The sun was rising and the village was slowly awakening when there was a scream from a young woman who was on her way to the river.

'Halala, Dumile and Bhatom are here! What a beautiful miracle this is! To escape from man-eating ogres in the middle of the night! Today I have seen it all.' She kept shouting until everyone was awake.

His parents and the whole village welcomed Dumile back home. And they all marvelled at the magic powers of the brave ox Bhatom for many years after that.

Cosi, cosi, iyaphela

HERE I REST MY STORY

QUEEN of the TORTOISES

Illustrations by Kalle Becker

THERE WAS ONCE a very big forest in Africa, where many, many kinds of animals lived. This was long ago, in the times when animals could still speak. Birds understood the language of animals and, in turn, the animals easily understood the different birdcalls that echoed through the forest.

Not very far from the forest, there was a big river where the animals went to drink. Times were good. There was lots of rain and plenty of food for everyone. So the different animals in the forest and on the surrounding plains were very happy.

But there was one little animal that did not feel so good about life. She was a young tortoise.

In those far off days the tortoise had a shell as smooth and plain as a hen's egg. For her, having enough food to eat and a place to sleep was not enough. She wanted more. She spent many hours thinking about her family and friends. To her they did not look very happy but they did not seem to want to do anything about it. The tortoise found life very unfair.

'Just look at the giraffe,' she thought to herself, 'so tall and elegant. Just look at the elephant – a whole mountain. I think the elephant must be the biggest animal in the world. I watch them all the time when they make their way to drink at the river. The king of all the animals – the lion – walks with confidence and looks so important with that beautiful mane around his powerful neck.'

'Just about everyone in and around the forest is good-looking or important for one thing or other – except us tortoises.'

'The cheetahs, the springboks – how fast they can run! The birds with their wonderful songs and their colourful feathers, especially the peacocks – how I would love to be as beautiful as the peacock.'

'Even the snakes that live around us on the ground are good to look at. If *only* I could have a shiny skin with lovely little patterns on it!'

'But the luckiest of all the reptiles must be the chameleon! Oh, to be able to change from one colour to the other any time I wish! *That* would make me the happiest tortoise in the whole world.'

These were the kinds of thoughts that filled the little tortoise's head for many days. She complained to her mother about her life, but her mother told her to try to accept herself as she was, because there was nothing she could do about it. The little tortoise tried to talk to her friends, but they carried on eating and slowly moving about, without paying much attention to what she was saying. This made her even sadder. She would sit and talk to herself.

'Tortoises must be the most uninteresting animals that ever lived. Our ugly shells look like the sand and the rocks around us. The other animals don't even notice us crawling around like shifting rocks. We hardly make any sound, so we cannot call out and greet other animals. We are just boring, boring, *boring*!'

She cried so much when she thought of how unlucky she was that she could hardly see straight. But she was also thinking about what she could do to improve her life. The thought of being a dirty, little tortoise for the rest of her days was unbearable. She simply had to *do* something.

She was sitting watching the sunset with her mother one evening, when a thought came to her. What if she went to bathe in the river first thing the next morning? It would be really good to be clean for a change. Yes, that's exactly what she would do. But she was not going to tell her mother; she wanted it to be a surprise.

So, the next morning, the young tortoise was the first one to see daybreak.

She made her way to the river. Everything was so quiet. The morning star was still shining brightly. The sky was already beginning to turn a little orange – soon the sun would peep up from under the edge of the world.

When the tortoise arrived at the river she decided to sit in the shallow water and soak herself for a while. Her feet and shell were submerged in the water; only her head showed. She strained her neck to look at her feet and shell, all ripply in the clear water. It made her laugh, but it felt good.

After a while she crawled out of the water. She rubbed and rubbed her shell against a sandy bank and also cleaned her feet with the sand before going back into the water. She did this a few times until she thought she was clean enough for one day. She washed her face and rinsed off all the sand and then she went to sit on a flat rock to dry. The warmth of the morning sun felt wonderful on her shell.

Later she walked home feeling very good about herself. She was smiling away as she passed two squirrels chasing each other up and down a tree. She expected them to notice her clean shell, but they carried on with their game and hardly gave her a second look. At home her brothers and sisters noticed that she had had a bath, but they were not at all impressed. They carried on playing in the dirt. Her mother thought it was all right, if it made her happy, but she warned her about crocodiles at the river.

'And crocodiles,' she commented, 'look so dirty although they live in the water. I don't know why you bother.'

But the young tortoise had made up her mind that she wanted to be different and being clean was the only difference she could think of. She really liked being the only clean tortoise around. Every morning she went to have her bath in the river and soon made friends with two ducks.

They had watched her polishing her shell and she had admired the way they glided easily on the water, still keeping their feathers dry and glossy. She asked them why they lived in the water when they could fly. She told them she would much prefer to fly than to swim. The ducks said they liked to do both. They had their nests on the riverbank and found food easily in the water.

The young tortoise moved around a lot. She wanted as many animals as possible to see her clean shell. When asked how come she was so clean, she proudly replied that she was a very special tortoise. But after a while she became bored with just being clean. She wanted more.

She knew that the animals all had group leaders. The lion was the supreme king of the forest animals. The paramount chief of the birds was the eagle who flew the highest of them all.

But when she looked at her own group – the boring reptiles – they did not seem to have a leader at all (unless it was the python). And, as far as she could see, they did not seem to care.

'Well,' she thought, 'it is time we also thought of having leaders, and why shouldn't it start with the tortoises?' (And, after all, wasn't *she* the cleanest tortoise around?)

From that day on she went around telling anyone who cared to listen that they should start respecting tortoises. 'We have a leader now,' she said. Asked who that leader was, she quickly answered: 'It's me. Can't you tell *I'm* the cleanest tortoise around here?'

Other tortoises soon heard that the young tortoise that went bathing every morning also claimed to be their leader. They thought her silly but it did not bother them as they knew that she meant no harm. (And, after all, the python could quickly crush anything that got out of hand.)

At first the young tortoise was very happy being a leader. But before long she began to wonder if it was really enough. She needed recognition. She asked herself: 'What do leaders do?'

But she could not answer that question (and she was too proud to ask anyone) so she went around listening when groups of animals were sitting together. She would sit very quietly so that they almost forgot she was there.

She listened to everything and everyone. And soon enough, she did find out what leaders did – they went to meetings!

How easy! She should have thought of it before! Now

she could just call a meeting of all the tortoises . . . no, that was not such a good idea. What would she say to them? She had never been to a meeting before. Hmm . . . right, she would wait to hear when the next meeting would be. She would learn from the other animals what they did at meetings and then she could come back and call all the tortoises to a meeting.

It was not long before she heard about the next meeting for all the leaders of different animals. It was to be held the very next day. She thought that was wonderful . . . until she heard where the meeting would be held.

It was at a place across the river. And the river was so big and wide – how was she to get to the other side in time? She was so slow; the meeting would be over long before she got there. She was very worried. Maybe that was why tortoises never bothered to have a leader – they knew they could not get to meetings!

The little tortoise knew she had to think of something – it was not right to give up so easily. Besides, everyone would laugh at her if she were not present at the leaders' meeting. It was very important for her to be there.

Then she thought of her good friends, the ducks. Maybe they could help her. So off she went, as fast as her short little legs could carry her, to the riverbank. The ducks saw her coming; they greeted her happily, but soon realised that something was troubling her.

'Dear friends, I need your help. I need to cross the river. There is a very important meeting of all the leaders, and as you know I am the leader of the tortoises. I have to be there. Please help me.'

She had the saddest expression on her face and the ducks felt very sorry for her. They tried to comfort her, saying they would find a way to help her. Swimming was not the thing to do. The river was too wide and there were crocodiles to worry about. Then one of the ducks had an idea – they could fly! If they held a strong stick in their bills and the tortoise held on between them they could easily fly her to the meeting – provided she did not open her mouth while they were in the air.

That evening a very happy tortoise went home, so excited she could hardly fall asleep. As she lay awake she decided that she was too special to be just a leader. After all, who had ever heard of a flying tortoise? The very next day she was going to make history. She was going to fly to the meeting. The title 'leader' was not good enough for her. She decided to call herself the Queen of the Tortoises. Yes, that sounded much better!

So the next morning, the self-appointed leader, now turned Queen of the Tortoises, woke up early and set off to have the most important bath of her life. She did not want the tiniest bit of dirt weighing her down as she flew to the meeting. Even the soles of her feet had to be clean. The other animals would be looking up at her and she knew they would laugh if her feet were dirty. She soaked and scrubbed and rinsed until she was exhausted. Then she sat there, smiling, and the rising sun seemed to be smiling back at her.

'Good morning, sun,' she whispered. 'You are the Ruler of the Skies, but did you know that I'm a Queen? I'm the Queen of the Tortoises!' She chuckled as the sun kept on smiling and getting warmer, but it did not reply. The ducks found her sitting on that flat rock, smiling away. They had to agree that she was the cleanest tortoise they had ever seen. She told them that she was no longer the leader of the tortoises, but she was now Queen of the Tortoises.

The ducks thought she deserved to be Queen, but it all depended on her. If she kept quiet the whole time they flew, she would make a Queen's entrance at the meeting.

Otherwise, they explained, if she let go of the stick she would fall down and crash to a painful death. She promised that whatever happened she would keep her mouth shut.

And so the Queen of the Tortoises stood between the two ducks. All three held onto the stick very tightly and with a few mighty flaps of the ducks' wings, the three friends rose up into the air. The tortoise had never thought that flying could feel so good. The wind under her feet and inside her shell felt wonderful. She could not believe how lucky she was. She wanted to fly over the forest first so that everyone could see her.

So the three friends flew up high over the forest and the morning sun shone on them and made them look really beautiful when the other animals noticed them.

The elephant was the first one to see them and she thought it was the strangest thing she had ever seen. She called out to alert the other animals and they all looked up. What miracle was this – a flying tortoise? The other tortoises also strained their necks to see what was going on in the sky. Their shells did not make it easy to look!

Because the ducks and tortoise were so high, the thin stick could not be seen from below. All the animals saw was two ducks flying with a tortoise. She moved her feet so gracefully, almost as if she were swimming. It looked as if she was flying easily with her friends.

The sounds of surprise and wonder coming from below filled the tortoise's heart with indescribable pride. She knew that at the meeting there would be no better news than that of a flying tortoise. But she forgot her promise to the ducks.

She just had to tell everyone that she was flying because she was Queen of the Tortoises. Her foolish pride made her open her mouth and shout down: 'I am the Queen! Queen of the . . . the . . . Tortoiseeeeeeeeeeeeeeees!' She could not say anything else as she was falling very fast.

Her horrified friends, the ducks, and all the other animals watched her come crashing down onto the hard ground. Her shell cracked into many pieces and she was badly hurt. She hid her head in her broken shell. Her pride was wounded worst of all.

For many days she stayed at home while her shell mended. Her mother and her friends fetched healing herbs and leaves and other tortoises came to visit every day. They told her that she could be Queen of the Tortoises any time she wanted, but she should understand that tortoises were never meant to fly. She promised everyone that she would not try again.

One day she decided to go to the river. She was missing the ducks and had not had a bath for some time. As she stood at the water's edge looking at her reflection, she realised that something wonderful had happened to her shell.

The cracks were mending and the segments were forming beautifully shaped patterns. The pieces had also acquired some colour from the herbs and leaves used to heal the wounds – a faint, greenish yellow could be seen. The Queen of the Tortoises was the very first tortoise to have a shell with patterns on it. She looked at herself and she was *very* pleased. The Queen looked very beautiful indeed!

Cosi, cosi, iyaphela

HERE I REST MY STORY

TIE ME UP!

Illustrations by Lalelani Mbhele

Here is a story I heard. It happened a very long time ago.

IN THOSE LONG AGO times when the rains came on time every year, there was more food than the animals could eat. Their skins were shiny. Their eyes were bright with good life and satisfaction. In fact, everything was so perfect that the animals grew lazy and fat. They thought that life would continue like this forever!

But that is not how life goes. One year the rains did not come for a whole four months. Then another six months went past without rain, and then the animals lost count as the sun continued to bake the earth. The rivers went dry; the grass and leaves dried up too and there was nothing left to eat.

Every morning the animals woke up and looked at the sky for a sign of one cloud, or maybe two . . . that would be promise enough of some relief. But day after day, the sky remained blue and the sun seemed to have come down even lower. Sometimes there would be terrible dust storms that left a huge area covered in a blanket of fine dust.

Many animals grew thin and died from thirst and hunger. Birds, reptiles and all kinds of animals were so thin and weak they doubted that they would see another day. Now life was about looking for water to drink, even a few drops would do, even if there was no food.

'This is no way to live! Without water our world is coming to an end!' a kudu was heard saying.

'I wish I was a migrating bird!' moaned Ostrich sadly.

Small animals looked at the bigger ones and thought: 'If only I was bigger and stronger then things would be better for me.' And the bigger animals wished to be smaller or at least be able to remove their horns and tusks for a while, until the rains returned.

One morning Giraffe and Elephant woke up very early. They had hardly slept really, because of the hunger eating away at their stomachs all night.

'My friend, today we walk east and we do *not* stop until we find food or water,' said Giraffe.

'East it is, my good friend, and it is today or never,' Elephant replied, pointing his trunk to the orange sky where the sun was about to rise.

The two animals walked and walked, crossing dry riverbed after dry riverbed, climbing hills and passing plains with groups of vultures looking at them with greedy eyes.

It was just after midday and their shadows were shortest under them, when they passed a little stream where they found a bit of water. The two

friends looked at each other and knelt down to drink and drink and drink! What a relief – their eyes could open a little wider. Their hearts began to beat a song of hope.

And then they looked up, and there – right there in front of them – was a big garden enclosed with very thick bushes. Inside were all kinds of fruit trees, heavy with ripe, juicy fruit. The delicious smell alone was enough to give the two friends new energy. They could feel their lips remembering how to smile again. Many, many different vegetables were growing in abundance in this special garden. The two friends asked themselves how it could be that a place like this existed and they did not know about it.

Giraffe, tall animal that he was, stretched his long neck and tried to grab a ripe peach.

Before he could even touch the fruit, they heard a terrifying voice. 'Grrrrrrrr! Hey! What do you think you are doing? Don't you dare touch that peach!'

Giraffe felt his whole body freeze from fear.

The voice came from a huge, red and black monster! It was Rhamuncwa! His eyes were blazing like fire with anger. His sharp teeth were the most scary the two friends had ever seen. His mouth was dripping saliva.

But Elephant had to try to talk sense to this greedy, terrifying creature.

'Please let us have a few pieces of fruit. We have not eaten in more than a week!' he pleaded.

'Get away from here before I kill you both, do you hear me? You are not getting one little *berry*. This is my garden! Everything in it is mine, and mine alone!' roared the ugly monster. His powerful body, sharp teeth and thunderous voice terrified even Elephant who was hungry and weak.

So the two friends walked away with their tails between their legs. The walk back home was even longer and more tiring. It was almost sunset when they got back and told all the other animals what they had seen.

The other animals were suddenly hopeful for a good meal, but then Giraffe and Elephant told them about the terrifying, greedy Rhamuncwa, so they all sat there feeling sorry for themselves. Their stomachs were growling together making a very sad song.

And then they heard a very different sound, a happy song coming down the hill. It was Nogwaja the Hare! He had a spring to the way he hopped along. He was looking so good! His skin was shining like he had never heard of the word 'Hunger'!

When he saw all the sad animals Nogwaja began to laugh and laugh.

'What is it with you lot? How did you all get so thin and so gloomy?'

A tired old lion looked at this rude little animal and he was annoyed. His mouth was watering as he had not eaten in days.

'Nogwaja, it is not funny. We might look funny to you but this time of hunger has been terrible on all of us. So watch what you say!'

Nogwaja saw that he was in danger and he apologised. Then the animals told him what had happened that day and about the greedy monster. Nogwaja smiled. 'This monster needs to meet *me*. I am the trickster of all tricksters! I will show him that not sharing, and being a bully, is a sign of weakness.'

'How will you do that?' asked the animals, confused.

'We are going to work together and make a strong rope. I have a plan. We will wake up early tomorrow and go to show that monster what we are made of,' Nogwaja said mysteriously.

* * *

When they arrived at the big garden the next day, the animals went in quietly, first the little ones, then the bigger ones and then the biggest. Nogwaja divided them into groups and told them what to do. Some climbed the trees and shook the branches. Bigger ones moved and shook the trunks of the trees, making a lot of noise.

Others jumped up and down and called loudly: 'Tie me up! Please, Nogwaja, tie me up!'

The owner of the garden woke up and roared angrily: 'What is all this noise in my garden?'

Nogwaja stepped forward. 'Are you still here? Haven't you heard that the world is coming to an end? I have to tie all those animals to tree-trunks so they will not be blown away by the great wind.'

Rhamuncwa was horrified at this news. 'Tie them up? Tie *them* up? No, that is not good. Start with me. Forget all those other fools. Tie me up!' he demanded. 'Tie *me* up first!'

Nogwaja pretended to be confused and scared.

'Hurry up and tie me up first before I eat you up!' shouted the monster, already standing on his hind legs up against the trunk of a tree.

Nogwaja took the rope and began tying up the ugly creature. When he thought he was finished the monster still wasn't happy. 'That is not good enough!' he roared. 'Do it tighter!'

So Nogwaja tied him really tightly, with Baboon helping him. The ugly Rhamuncwa could not move anything but his eyes.

Then the great trickster jumped back and called to the others: 'Stop the noise good friends; now let's eat!'

How happy the other animals were. For once Nogwaja had done something really good. Everyone thanked him while they ate and ate – and while they also enjoyed themselves, laughing and teasing the monster who could do nothing to stop them.

After they had all had enough food, Nogwaja asked the animals to take all the seeds from the garden and store them carefully. When the rains came again, they could grow their *own* food in their *own* gardens – and freely share with one another the fruits and vegetables they grew.

That is what they did. They worked happily, planting those new gardens. And when the rains finally came, the new gardens began to grow beautifully.

And the monster? He escaped one night and was never seen in those parts again.

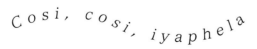

Cosi, cosi, iyaphela

HERE I REST MY STORY

MOONLIGHT MAGIC

Illustrations by Suset Maakal

Nolitha WAS A HAPPILY married woman. Her husband was a great warrior and he was well respected in the community.

Many people spoke about him, saying: 'He is fearless! He spits in the face of death!'

But his loving wife Nolitha did not like fighting of any kind. She wished for a time when nobody needed to be a brave warrior for any reason. She feared for her husband's life every time he went into battle.

'You must not worry so much. I will always come back to you, my lovely Nolitha,' he often said.

But one day the thing she feared most happened. He was one of the first men to be killed in a surprise attack by a village they had defeated not so long ago. All the people were so sad to lose such a powerful fighter. Nolitha was in more pain than she had ever thought possible. She missed him so much. And they did not have a single child yet. How she longed to have a baby.

The people of her village knew how much she loved children and the children also loved her. When they had finished their chores at home, they went to Nolitha's house. She sang with them, played clap rhythms with them and told them happy stories. It was hard for them to go home in the evenings. But she promised them that next time they would have more fun; for now they had to go home to their parents.

Nolitha was not happy inside. When she was alone she wept for her beloved man and wished he was still alive. She wanted so much to have a child of her own. Most nights she dreamt of this. Sometimes she could not fall asleep as she lay in bed imagining what it would be like to be a mother.

It was one such night when she decided to do something about her problem. It was a quiet summer night. The stars twinkled like many happy eyes in the night sky. And the moon was so bright as it washed the land in its silvery glow. Nolitha put on her best clothes and most beautiful, beaded necklace and bracelets and anklets. Her orange hat also had beads decorating it. She looked really beautiful.

Then she set out and walked to the river, to the part where the waterfall was the loudest. It was a pleasant walk and at midnight she knew everyone was asleep. When she finally stood up on a rock overlooking the waterfall, the roaring water was almost magical with the bright moonlight dancing on it. This was the exact place where she had met her husband, one summer evening, so many years ago. She looked up at the moon and smiled, and then she opened her mouth to sing – a song that was like a prayer:

Mpophoma nawe Nyanga!
Ngiyazithoba kinina
Ngicelingane, Hemh! Hemh!

Oh Waterfall and you Moon!
I humble myself before you
Asking for a baby, Hemh! Hemh!

She sang her song for a long time and a gentle breeze carried the song all over the sleeping village. She went on singing till she was too tired to sing any more. Then she went back home to sleep.

The people who heard the beautiful sound were not sure if it was part of a sweet dream they had dreamed. But it was such a lovely sound that it stayed with them all day as they did their work. A villager would be heard humming the melody of the song to a neighbour. And they would be surprised that they both knew the melody but not the words of the song.

'I think someone was singing for me in a dream last night,' said one woman.

'Hey, me too! I think I dreamed about someone singing this lovely song just outside my window.'

They continued with their work and the melody slowly faded after a few days.

Next time there was a full moon, Nolitha waited until it was midnight and then went out of her house beautifully dressed as if she was going to a special wedding. If her husband were still alive or if the villagers had seen her like that they would have marvelled at her beauty. She walked to the same place and stood at the top of the waterfall and listened to its powerful song. She admired its magically silver glow as the moonlight danced on its waters. Like the last time, she smiled at the moon and began to sing:

Mpophoma nawe Nyanga!
Ngiyazithoba kinina
Ngicelingane, Hemh! Hemh!

Oh Waterfall and you Moon!
I humble myself before you
Asking for a baby, Hemh! Hemh!

She sang for a long time . . . pleading . . . longing for a little baby of her own. She sang from the bottom of her heart and a gentle breeze carried the song all over the sleeping village. She went on singing until she was too tired to sing any more. And then she went back home to sleep.

Tired yes, but feeling good inside, she slept soundly that night. She had a beautiful dream where she was a young girl playing with other children as they swam under the waterfall. It was such a lovely dream she did not want to wake up.

But then she was awoken by a very distinct sound – the sound of a baby crying. No, it could not be! She threw off her blanket and went to open the door.

Yes, it was a baby! Unbelievable. 'Whose baby could it be?' she wondered. She looked outside, to the left and then to the right. Nobody. The baby was sitting inside a huge dug-out pumpkin as if it had grown in the garden. Nolitha looked at the little face and the big, round eyes looked right up at her. The baby smiled and made gurgling noises. Nolitha decided that the moonlight magic must have worked. Her prayers had been answered. The moon and the waterfall had responded to her singing. They had heard her plea and finally decided to give her a baby of her own.

Nolitha took the baby inside the house and closed the door behind her. She washed him and gave him some creamy milk porridge with honey. She marvelled at his little hands, tiny fingers and toes – his sweet smile and those big, round eyes that looked like small moons.

Nolitha was the happiest she had been in all her life. She could not stop smiling and humming her song. But she was careful not to make any noise. She wished to enjoy that baby alone, even if it was only for one day. You see, she was still thinking that somebody would come to ask if she had found their baby.

She did not leave her house that day. The next day she stayed indoors for the whole day too, and at night went outside to fetch water, get some vegetables from her garden and bring in some firewood.

From that day onwards, Nolitha slept in the daytime with the baby, played

quietly when he awoke, and then put him back to sleep when he was tired. Then at night she did her work in secret. Days went by and the neighbours wondered where Nolitha had gone. The village children came looking for her but she kept quiet and did not answer their calls.

But after some time she decided that it was all right to tell people about her new baby. Surely it would be impossible to live like this forever? It was the children who first noticed that her door was open and Nolitha was sitting outside by the door. They came closer and when they saw the baby they ran to greet her.

'Sawubona mama Nolitha! We have not seen you for a long time,' said the first child.

'And the baby, oh he is so beautiful! What is his name?'

'Please can I hold him? I promise I will not drop him.'

Nolitha laughed at all their questions and also because she was relieved to see her young friends again. She had not realised how wonderful it would be to share her baby with others.

'His name is Njabulo. I named him that because he has brought me so much joy,' she said, as she saw more neighbours coming to her house one after the other.

They could not believe their eyes and ears. But they were all happy to see her again. They sat and talked for a long time, admiring the baby boy and making funny sounds that made him laugh. Then everybody laughed out loud and it seemed they all wanted to hold that baby.

Nolitha's world was complete. The moonlight magic had done it for her. She knew it would be her greatest pleasure to raise her little boy, Njabulo, in a village filled with so many caring people. And the other children would be like his brothers and sisters too.

Cosi, cosi, iyaphela

HERE I REST MY STORY

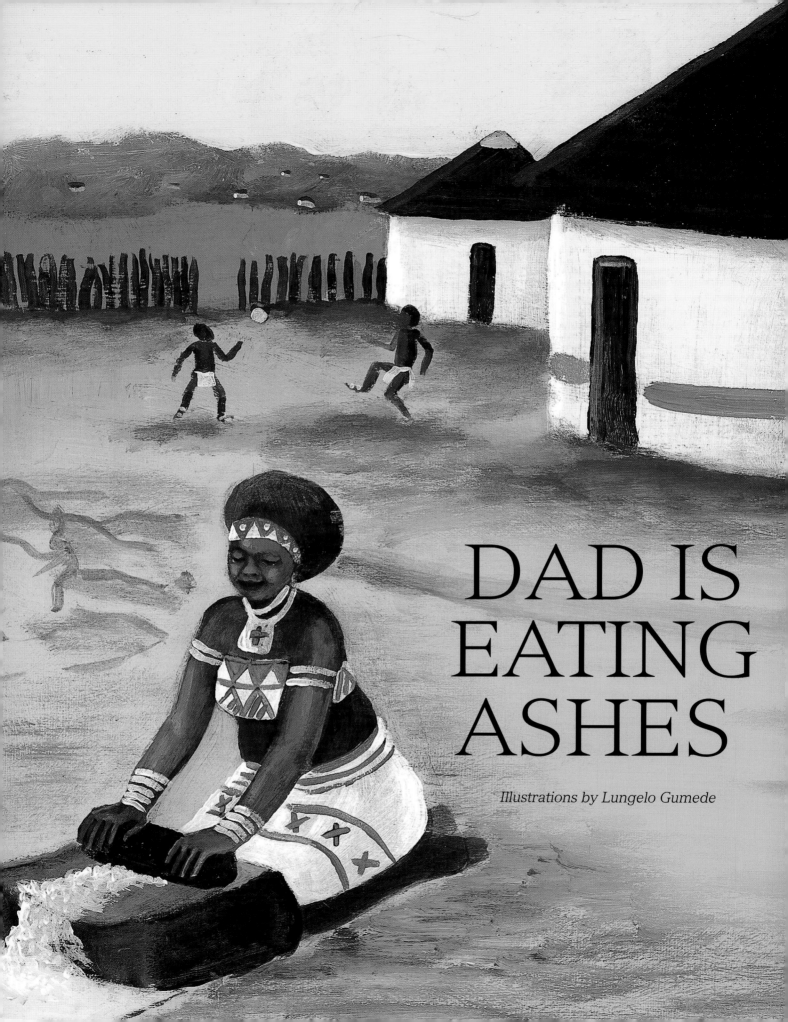

DAD IS EATING ASHES

Illustrations by Lungelo Gumede

THERE WAS ONCE a man called Zangwa who lived with his family. Zangwa was quite respected in his community and so was his wife, who made the most beautiful clay pots. Many people admired her work. Zangwa and his wife had a happy family with four children – three boys and a girl.

The chief of that village was a kind man. Many villagers also thought he was a wise man too. At big meetings the chief would address everyone.

'My people,' he would say, 'we must always remember to celebrate the good times together and support one another in hard times. Because, just as the sun rises and goes down every day, the good and bad times always find their way into our lives.'

Old people nodded their heads. 'He speaks the truth, our chief.'

One year the people of that village suffered the worst drought they had experienced in years. The sun was so hot that people did not know where to hide. Zangwa and his wife woke up every day and went to work in the fields, tilling the land. This way the water would go deep into the ground when the rains finally came. The children also helped but sometimes the sun was too much for them.

When Zangwa's wife walked home, she picked some wild spinach and used a digging stick to pull out some roots they could eat for supper. Often that was all they ate for days.

The oldest child grumbled, 'I do not like these strange roots we have to eat. I wish the rains would come. Then some real food could grow in the fields.' The others agreed. They ate only to chase away the hunger, not because they liked the taste of the food.

One day Zangwa was working in the fields with his wife and children. He looked up and saw a bird. It was a honey

guide and it was calling urgently. He dropped his hoe and shouted, 'I think I should follow that bird. I think it is inviting me to go and find some honey!'

The children's faces lit up. They could imagine the honeycomb their father was going to bring back later that day. Their mother smiled to herself as she saw the look on the children's faces.

'Yes, I think you should go. Take one of the clay pots at home and bring back some juicy honeycomb for us!' she said. The day was promising. There was going to be a special treat for a change.

Zangwa followed the honey guide for some time. The bird led him to the edge of the forest and stopped. Soon he saw there were lots of bees buzzing around one very big tree.

'So this is it. We have found the beehive. Thank you beautiful bird!' So saying, Zangwa quickly made a fire under the tree and the bees flew away. They hated the smoke coming up to their nest.

Now Zangwa could climb up to the big branch where the honey was shining golden in the midday sun. One by one he pulled out the honeycombs. They were dripping with honey and he easily filled the pot he had brought with him. He also put one thick piece on a flat rock for the bird that had helped him.

'Thank you my friend; these are delicious!' he said to the bird.

The bird ate heartily. And next to it Zangwa squeezed the honeycombs until only the golden liquid honey filled the pot almost to the top. He ate some and then licked his fingers clean.

'What a wonderful feeling, to touch, smell and eat

this special food for the gods!' he said to himself, smiling from ear to ear. He picked up the pot and started to make his way home.

He had not gone far when suddenly he stopped and thought, 'This honey is too good to be wasted. If I share it with my wife and four children it will be finished immediately. But if I hide it and eat it alone it will last for a few days . . .'

He took a few more slow steps and then stopped again. 'Mmmhhh! Yes, I know what to do. I will wash my face and hands clean at the stream. There will be no smell of honey left. Then I will go home and hide the honey where no one will even think of looking. I will tell them that the bird flew away and left me with no beehive in sight.'

His mind was made up. On his way back home he washed himself. He found a place to hide the honey from his family. He dug a hole in the place where they threw old ashes, put the pot in there and covered it with a flat piece of wood. Quickly he made a small hole in the middle of the wood. He then went to get a reed straw with which to suck the honey. Now all that was left was to cover the spot with more ashes.

Zangwa went back to the fields walking slowly, looking sad and tired.

'Father, what is wrong?' asked his daughter.

'That bird made a fool of me. There was no honey . . .' he answered in a sad voice.

The oldest child stamped his foot. 'Oh no, I hate this! We have not had honey for so long. We should have gone with you to help you look.'

Their mother kept quiet. She looked for other roots and herbs for the family to eat.

When the family sat down for supper that evening, Zangwa turned to his wife and said, 'Please do not dish up for me. There is so little food in the pot. You can eat with the children; I will eat ashes.'

The children were shocked, and so was their mother.

'No, you can eat as well. We always eat together, no matter how little food is in the pot,' Zangwa's wife pleaded with him. But he would not change his mind.

'I am a big man. I can miss a meal sometimes, but the children need the food more.'

In this way he started pretending that he was eating ashes to sacrifice for the sake of his wife and children. He went to the ash heap and knelt down. He took the reed straw and placed it in his mouth. Slowly he sucked the delicious honey, but his face was a mask of pain. It was as if he was eating something very bitter.

Then he called his children to come and dance around him, singing, 'Dad is eating ashes! Dad is eating ashes!'

The children sang and clapped their hands as they laughingly danced around their father. They thought it was all a crazy game.

Their mother stood at the door and watched, confused.

The next day Zangwa did not eat again.

'No, do not dish up for me, I will try to eat ashes again,' he said.

The children ate quickly and went to sing for their father. 'Dad is eating ashes! Dad is eating ashes!' they clapped their hands and sang over and over.

This went on for days on end, and sometimes the children called their friends to come and play the game with them. There was much dancing and laughing as the children sang around Zangwa.

After four days of this game the woman secretly went to look at the ash heap when her husband was not there. She scratched away carefully. Then she lifted the flat piece of wood. The straw was still there and the smell was inviting. She saw the pot and lifted it up. She could not believe her eyes!

'A pot of honey! So these are the ashes he has been hiding away from us!'

Quickly the woman found another hiding place for the pot and covered it with some dry grass, then sand . . . and next to it she put a big stone to mark the place for the future.

That evening the man came home and sat outside on his wooden bench. Again he did not want to eat with the family.

After supper he called to the children, 'Come and sing for me.'

They jumped up and started dancing around their father. This was such a strange game. But it was fun too.

Zangwa took the straw and put it in his mouth as usual. With a painful look on his face he sucked what he thought was his honey. But real ashes came into his mouth. They tasted terrible! He shook his head from side to side, spitting all over the place. Confused, Zangwa tried to suck again but more ashes filled his mouth. From the doorway his wife smiled secretly. The children kept on singing until he shouted at them.

'Stop it! I have had enough of this. Every day ashes, ashes, ashes!' he shouted angrily.

The children did not understand what was going on. But their father went into the house and asked his wife for some leftover food.

'There is nothing left, I am sorry,' she said quietly. 'For days now you have been eating ashes . . .'

'Well, I have had enough ashes! Can't you understand that?' shouted her husband.

With his finger he licked the bottom of the pot and drank some water before going to bed.

After that he never wanted to eat ashes again. When the children asked, 'Can we sing for you again, father?' he told them to leave him alone.

After some time the rains came. The people of the village planted sweet potatoes, mealies, green and brown beans, millet, pumpkins and other food. Life went back to normal again. The harvest was really good too.

And then it was time to have a big End Of Harvest celebration at the chief's place. Everyone put on their best clothes. Girls and women made new hairstyles and put beads around their necks. They looked beautiful. There was so much food it was hard to think that not even a year ago the people had been going to bed with hungry stomachs. But they remembered those days. They shared stories of how they had survived.

'We even ate frogs,' one man told his friends.

'Oh, we ate strange mushrooms and we got so sick I thought we would die!' said another woman.

'At our house it was different. My husband really sacrificed more than anyone I know,' said Zangwa's wife.

'What did he do?' asked the people.

'He did not eat the little food we had; instead, he ate ashes,' she said.

Now everyone was listening.

'Hawu! What a strong man Zangwa is!' exclaimed his friends and neighbours.

'Yes, he is. He even asked the children to sing for him when he ate ashes,' she continued.

'Yes, it is true,' agreed the children, and their friends too.

But Zangwa's wife was not finished. She rushed to her secret place and dug up the pot of honey. She brought it back and placed it in front of the chief.

'These are the ashes my husband ate while the children sang and danced around him,' she said.

Zangwa could not move. He looked down and wished that the ground would open up and swallow him.

Everyone stood up and looked. What a shock they got when they saw what was inside the pot. The disgust on their faces was unspeakable. The chief was quiet for a long time. Then he stood up, looking at the embarrassed man in front of him.

'Zangwa!' he called, 'I do not want to hear a word from you. I want you to stand up and walk away from this village. What you have done is terrible. You should really be ashamed of yourself. You will not be welcomed back here for six months. Maybe by that time you will have had a change of heart. You can only come back when you have learned to be a more caring man. When you can teach your children about sharing, love and respect. At the moment, you do not have any of those. So go. Right now!'

Zangwa could not even look at his children or his wife. He walked away as fast as he could – not knowing where to go.

Days and nights he walked. The news of the man who pretended to eat ashes spread to other villages too. So he was not welcome in many homes. Those were the most painful months for him.

But he did learn his lesson and when he returned to his village he was more caring than he had ever been in his life before. The chief and all his neighbours welcomed him back. His wife and children forgave him and they enjoyed many wonderful years together.

But many people told his story for years after that. Everywhere Zangwa went he heard the word 'ashes' – and tasted them in his mouth too!

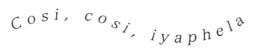

HERE I REST MY STORY

MAMBA
ka
MAQHUBA

Illustrations by Suset Maakal

THOBEKA AND BUSI were sisters. They lived with their parents in a small village. Life was very quiet in their village and Thobeka enjoyed that life. She was a gentle, hard-working girl. Each morning, first thing when she woke, she cleaned the house and fetched water from the river. Sometimes she watered the plants that needed more water when there was not enough rain. Her parents were proud of the vegetable garden. The sweet potatoes, beans, millet and pumpkins were looking as happy as Thobeka was.

But Thobeka's sister Busi was rude and did not care what other people thought or said about her. She did whatever she wanted exactly when she wanted. She did not help around the house either. Oh, and she enjoyed eating and resting under the shade of a tree and dreaming away.

'All that hard work and sweating is for fools! I need to relax and take good care of myself. I am too beautiful to be playing with dirt and weeds in the garden,' she often said when her younger sister Thobeka asked her to help.

'Busi, you should try just once and you will feel the joy of helping life grow.'

'What nonsense you speak! Leave me alone please!' Busi replied irritably.

Thobeka continue to work happily in the vegetable garden. She sang and felt like she was part of the choir of the many birds that chirped merrily in the trees around her home.

Sometimes it seemed the birds were lonely when she was not there. When she returned from gathering firewood in the forest or fetching water from the river, her parents would say to her: 'Thank you, Thobeka. Now you can take your food and drink outside so the birds can know you are back. They have missed you all morning.'

She would laugh. 'But they know exactly where I was! Some of them were there with me and the other girls. I recognised their voices.'

Even garden snakes seemed to look forward to her singing. Busi ran for her life if she saw the smallest garden snake, but Thobeka knew they meant no harm at all.

One day the news came that their king was inviting all the girls in the land to come and meet his son. The prince needed a wife. Many girls went off to the king's place. But, one by one, they came back all very nervous and not saying what had happened when they met the prince. Then Busi, the older sister, told her parents that she wanted to go and meet the prince.

'It is obvious that the prince has not seen me yet. I just know that he will want to marry me. So please, just be happy that your daughter is the one!' she boasted.

Thobeka prepared some travelling food and water for her sister. 'Go well, child of my father. I wish you good luck,' she said kindly.

'Do shut up! I need no good luck wishes from you,' Busi sneered, taking her provisions and leaving the house. She was already out of the gate when she turned and called out: 'Next time you see me, I will be your queen!' She laughed out loud and walked away, full of confidence. Her parents stood at the door shaking their heads, wondering how she got to be so proud and selfish.

On her way Busi met an old woman who spoke to her. 'Please, my child, can you come and help me to clean my eyes. I can hardly see anything,' she said.

'Wipe your own eyes and leave me alone,' came the sharp answer from Busi. But the old woman insisted. She tried to give Busi advice about what to expect on the way to the king's house.

'Soon you will come to a place with many trees with faces. They will laugh at you but please do not laugh back at them.'

Busi told her to leave her alone and went on her way. When she turned to look back the old woman had disappeared. 'How very strange,' she thought.

Not long after that she came to a part of the forest where all the trees had faces. They were laughing at her.

'Hahaha! I laugh back at you! Who do you think you are, laughing at your future queen? Hahaha! I laugh back at you!' said Busi, stamping her feet on the hard ground and walking past furiously.

Next she met a young boy with old, torn clothes standing in the middle of the path. He had his hand out. 'Please, sister, can you give me something to eat. I am very hungry,' he pleaded.

'The food I have here is enough for me alone. So go and get your own food. And you should know that I will soon be your queen and I do not need rude boys bothering me like this!' she snapped, and she walked away.

She had hardly taken two steps past when the boy simply vanished!

'What strange people these are!' Busi said to herself, but continued on her journey. She was getting very tired and hungry. She found a good place to sit and enjoy her meal. Then she stood up and walked on, hoping that the great place was not too far.

It was late afternoon when she made it to the king's kraal. She greeted everyone with a cool air of self-importance. 'Come this way,' said one young woman. Busi was led into a big, round hut and told to grind the millet on a grinding stone and prepare a meal for the prince.

'But where is he? I want to see him!' Busi demanded.

'Please be patient. You will see him tonight when he returns,' said the young woman and left her alone.

Busi did not know how to grind millet properly. At her home Thobeka always did that sort of work. But Busi did what she could and made soft porridge for the prince. Then she sat and waited.

It was late at night and everything was quiet. She was almost falling asleep when she heard a strange sound coming closer and closer to the hut. Busi's eyes opened wide with fear and she jumped to the far end of the hut.

The door suddenly opened and a big mamba snake came in. 'Greetings to you. I am the prince. Have you prepared anything for me to . . .'

But he could not finish. Busi was screaming so loudly, and shaking from head to toe, that he couldn't even get the words out.

As soon as she could Busi ran out of the door and did not stop all night until she made it home early the next morning.

Her beautiful face swollen from crying and exhaustion, she told her family what had happened. 'And please do not go there, Thobeka. That snake prince will eat you alive!' she said, crying uncontrollably. Her little sister had never seen proud Busi so very scared.

'But I am not scared. I want to try as well. Maybe he will want to marry me,' Thobeka said, smiling gently.

'If you are that dumb then go! Maybe he should marry the ugly sister!' Busi shouted as she ran to her hut.

Thobeka asked her parents if she could go. They agreed and helped her to get ready. Early the next morning Thobeka set off. Her parents wished her well and reminded her that they were proud of the daughter she was.

On her way Thobeka met the same old woman that Busi had seen before. 'Please, my child, can you help me to clean my eyes? I can hardly see

anything.' Thobeka helped the old woman to clean her eyes. And she listened to the advice the old woman had to give.

'Soon you will come to a place with many trees with faces,' she said to Thobeka. 'They will laugh at you but please do not laugh back at them.'

'Thank you, grandmother,' she said respectfully when the old woman had finished.

'May good fortune always follow you, my child,' the old woman answered before she disappeared.

When Thobeka arrived at the place with many laughing trees she did not laugh back at them. She bowed respectfully and continued on her journey.

Then she suddenly saw a young boy standing in front of her begging for food. 'Come and share some of my food,' she said. 'Here is a sweet potato and here I have some delicious millet and fruit bread. I baked it myself.'

The young boy accepted the food and whispered a thank you before vanishing right in front of her eyes.

Thobeka knew this was no ordinary boy. But there was no fear in her heart. She smiled and continued on her journey.

Soon the king's kraal was visible up on a hill. It looked beautiful – so many big, round huts built of strong rocks with neatly thatched roofs. The whole place was shaped in a circle with one entrance facing east. The immaculately arranged sticks and boulders formed a protective wall around the village. There were many hundreds of cattle grazing in the valley near the great place. Thobeka was overwhelmed by it all. Slowly she walked towards the entrance. People saw her coming and they were watching carefully as she walked in. She greeted them politely.

The sisters of the prince liked her immediately. 'Welcome to our home! What is your name?' they asked.

'Thobeka,' she answered, smiling quietly. The sisters helped her by telling her what to do to win the prince's affection.

'Our brother was cursed many years ago. He was turned into a mamba snake. That is why he is called Mamba kaMaqhuba. But do not fear! He is the kindest man in the land. Stay calm when he returns later tonight and give him his food. If you are the one girl he falls in love with, you will help break the curse. Then he will turn back into a prince once more.'

Thobeka thanked them and took great care to grind the millet to the finest powder. She then made the most delicious, creamy porridge with milk and mixed into it some wild honey she had brought as a gift for the prince.

Later that night the strangest wind blew; there was howling, and scary sounds could be heard coming closer and closer. But Thobeka sat calmly and waited. She took a deep breath as the door opened and the big mamba snake came in and slithered slowly towards Thobeka.

'Greetings to you, beautiful maiden. I am Mamba kaMaqhuba, the prince.'

'Respectful greetings to you, my prince. I am happy to meet you.' She bowed her head and smiled at him. Then she placed the food in front of him and he enjoyed the meal she had cooked with so much tenderness. When he had finished, the snake prince thanked her. 'That was delicious! You cook very well,' he said, looking at her with kind eyes. 'Can I sit with you?'

When Thobeka nodded her head the mamba snake came closer and wrapped himself around her body. She let him wrap himself until his face was close to hers and they had a good look at each other. They stayed like this for hours, talking and laughing quietly together.

'Your heart is as beautiful as you are kind. Thank you for loving me even though I am a creature so many run away from,' he said, gazing into her eyes.

Slowly he unwrapped himself from her and coiled himself on the kudu skin next to her. They soon fell asleep. After so many experiences all in one day, Thobeka was happy to relax and sleep at last.

Very early the next morning a more gentle wind blew in under the door. A thin wisp of smoke came in with it and circled above the snake prince and the bad spell was then broken. Mamba kaMaqhuba became a very handsome young man once more.

He was sitting on a wooden stool smiling at her when Thobeka woke up.

'Good morning, my happiness! Love of my heart!' he greeted her, flashing the brightest white smile. Thobeka jumped up and ran to him. They held each other for a long time before they went out to share the good news with everyone in the royal family. There were screams of joy when the sisters and their mother saw Prince Mamba!

What a wonderful day! The spell was broken. The snake was no more. The air was filled with joyous singing and celebrating. Everyone wore a smile on their faces.

The old king and queen thanked Thobeka again and again.

'Now we know the next king and queen will be a very loving and caring pair. Our people are in good hands. May good fortune always follow you, my children,' they said.

Thobeka and her prince travelled to her home with many gifts and cattle and food. There were so many colourfully dressed people travelling with them and many more followed. The whole country knew that the prince had found his bride and everyone was welcome to celebrate their wedding, both at the bride's home and then back at the king's kraal.

And so began the married life of Thobeka and Prince Mamba kaMaqhuba, as he was known.

Many times he would take her hand, look into her eyes and whisper, 'Thank you, my happiness. Love of my heart!'

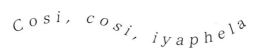

HERE I REST MY STORY

The SINGING DOG

Illustrations by Kalle Becker

ALONG TIME AGO different animals and birds all lived together. They went hunting together and they looked after their young. Lion had been their king from the very beginning – all the other animals respected and obeyed his word. Many animals also feared their king. Yet some said that the hare could have easily been chosen king, had he not been so small, as many animals feared the hare too.

Everyone agreed that he was a clever and cunning little creature although not very respectable. The springhare, in one way or another, had tricked countless animals and they were still thinking up ways of getting back at him. So nobody wanted to make friends with him. But Hare did not worry himself with all the bad talk that went around. He was quite satisfied with only one friend in the world. And this was the only animal he never teased. His best friend was Dog.

Dog and his friend Hare had all kinds of good times together as they went looking for food in the forest. They played games too; many times they raced each other (but it was soon decided that Dog was a little too fast for Hare, so they stopped playing *that* game). They even protected each other if there was any unexpected danger. They played hide and seek and they laughed a lot! An ordinary, boring winter morning would easily turn into a day filled with fun and adventure.

Yes, both friends liked playing some funny tricks on other animals but, apart from this, Hare and Dog were quite different animals.

Dog always tried not to hurt anybody; sometimes he played a clever trick on a cruel animal to save another. But his friend, Hare, would stop at *nothing*. As long as he had his fun, everything was all right by him – even if the game resulted in the injury or possibly death of another animal.

Many days Dog sat with his friend and tried to make him see that it was possible to have a huge amount of fun without hurting others. Hare only listened with one ear and went on with his ways. He just laughed at Dog. He knew in his heart that the only thing that really made him happy was to annoy, irritate and humiliate a much bigger animal and to strip away its dignity. Only Dog was safe from Hare's tricks.

It must be said that the two friends admired each other a lot. Hare was particularly fond of his friend because of his especially beautiful singing voice. Dog was the only animal that could sing. All the other animals made all sorts of sounds with their voices but they could not sing.

When the animals got together in their meetings called by King Lion – Dog would stand on a rock and sing out for all to hear. And what sweet songs he sang too! Even the birds came down to perch on some tree branches to listen to the singing dog. There would be silence all across the valleys and the plains. Every creature marvelled at the beauty of Dog's voice. Hare was very proud indeed. He told any animal that would listen that Dog was his best friend.

Well, one day Hare went away on his own all day. Dog did not know where his friend had disappeared to, and he missed him very much. When it got to be late afternoon, Dog began worrying and thinking about all the things that could have happened to Hare. He wondered if Hare had been caught and eaten by one of the big animals that hated him for his cruel tricks.

And then Hare came home – not walking, but humming and skipping as he approached. Relieved, Dog sat down and looked at him, wondering what story he was about to hear. He could see on Hare's face that he had enjoyed his day. Dog demanded to know where Hare had been. Hare simply stood in front of him with a big grin on his face – it stretched from ear to ear –

until Dog could not stand it any longer. He walked round and round Hare, his ears all pricked up. He was ready to listen when Hare finally spoke.

'Dog, my friend, how do I start telling you of the new feeling that is in my heart right now? It is pure joy!'

This made Dog even more impatient. 'Do say what has happened to you? I have never seen you so happy before.' He wished that Hare would just *speak up* and tell him everything at once!

'Dog, you will not believe this. I have spent this marvellous day with the most beautiful, the cleanest and cleverest pig you can imagine!'

'What are you saying to me? A pig? Beautiful, clean and clever?'

'I am telling you that I love her and she loves me.'

Dog could not speak for a moment. Since when did hares fall in love with pigs? Then he laughed.

'So you say you love her . . . I can see you are a changed hare – I have never seen you so happy before. And to think you did not humiliate anybody!'

'My friend, won't you *please* come with me tomorrow to visit her? I know you will agree with me that she is the *most* beautiful pig ever born.' Hare was almost begging his friend. This Dog found very unusual.

'To visit the prettiest pig in the land would be most enjoyable. I certainly will go with you, my friend!' he said, smiling at Hare teasingly.

So the next morning the two friends had a very quick breakfast and they began brushing each other's coats as they wanted to look good. Hare took extra care with his whiskers. All this was new and Dog watched him with great interest. Soon they were on their way. Hare walked ahead – his ears up in the air with excitement and his little tail gently bobbing along as he went.

Dog was close behind his friend – his tail up in the air and his long, red tongue hanging out as he trotted along. Off they went, off they went – now walking faster . . . and then faster . . . and then running a bit. Hare just could not take that smile off his face. 'I love her and she loves me. I love her and she loves me!' was all he could think of.

Finally they arrived at Pig's house. She was sitting quietly under a tree,

waiting. When Dog saw her for the first time, he had to agree with his friend – this surely was the prettiest pig ever born. When she saw them she stood up and gave them a big smile. She thought Hare looked so very handsome with his coat shining like that. And his eyes were the most intelligent eyes she had ever seen.

She offered them something to drink and she was introduced to Dog. They all rested under the shade of the tree. Immediately Hare and Pig sat down holding hands and looking into each other's eyes. They soon forgot all about Dog and the rest of the world. (Hmph! What world?) They chatted happily and did not even notice Dog as he quietly moved away from them. He went to sit on a rock nearby. He looked at his best friend with a funny new feeling. He had never seen him so happy before. He wanted to do something that would make him even happier. So he started to sing a song for him and Pig:

Ondibuzayo ndithanda bani
Ndakumxelela ndithanda yena
UHagwana wam.

Whoever will ask me who I love,
I'll tell them I love her
My only Piggy – Hagwana.

Hare was very pleased with his friend. Hagwana the pig, could not believe her clean little ears. She had never heard of a singing dog before. And what a sweet voice he had too! The three spent a very special day together. It was not easy to say goodbye to Hagwana the pig.

'Do you have to go?' she asked them. They promised to be back the next day.

That evening at supper, Hare could hardly taste his food. He had such a dreamy look in his eyes. And all they talked about was Pig, Pig, Pig. Dog noticed too that his friend had forgotten all about playing tricks and humiliating other animals. He was full of smiles and chuckled to himself each time he remembered a little joke they had shared with Hagwana.

But then after visiting Pig a few times and singing for them, Dog got tired of talking about her all the time. He really missed the adventures he and Hare had enjoyed before Hare met the prettiest pig in the land. He told his friend that he would not be going with him any more to visit Hagwana. Hare did not complain. He went alone to visit his loved one.

But the first question Hagwana asked was: 'Where is Dog?'

'What do you mean, "Where is Dog?" I am here and I love you,' Hare said, tickling her nose and trying not to show he was a little angry.

'Yes, I love you too and I'm happy to see you. But I really miss Dog with his beautiful singing,' she said shyly.

They sat down and talked and held hands. They laughed a few times and tried to be happy with each other, but something was just not right. They did not enjoy themselves as much as they did when Dog was there. Hare went home much earlier than he had planned. He did not like what was happening.

When he got home, Hare convinced Dog that he had to come along on the next visit. 'The road is twice as long when you are not there!' he told Dog.

Dog said he would go, but made Hare promise that they would not talk about Hagwana on the way *there* or *back*. Hare agreed, and so the very next day the two friends were on their way again. Pig was very happy to see them.

'Oh, Dog! You are here! Please sing for us,' she begged. So the two lovers sat holding hands and Dog sang:

Ondibuzayo ndithanda bani
Ndakumxelela ndithanda yena
UHagwana wam.

Whoever will ask me who I love,
I'll tell them I love her
My only Piggy – Hagwana.

Pig was most pleased. She held hands with Hare, but she only had eyes for Dog. Hare saw the look on her face, and it seemed to say: 'What an amazing creature this is!'

Hare was very angry and he felt cheated. For the first time in his life he hated his friend. He wanted to kick him hard between those trusting eyes. But he knew he had to keep on smiling. He thanked Dog for his song.

When the two friends got home they had a big supper at Hare's house. It was a beautiful summer evening. The moon was full and it washed the whole countryside with its cool, magical light. The stars twinkled happily at the two friends as they sat there with their stomachs all filled up. Then Hare suddenly sprang to his feet as if something had pinched him.

'My friend, Dog, I have a surprise for you,' he said.

'What is it?' asked Dog.

'Oh, it's a little something to thank you for everything you have done for me and Hagwana,' he said, not meeting Dog's eyes.

'But you are my friend; there's no need to thank me.'

'Don't say any more. I have some medicine right here; I got it yesterday. Everyone talks about your lovely voice but this medicine will make it even sweeter than honey. Wait a little bit; I'll go and fetch it.'

Hare disappeared behind a bush and came back holding something behind his back. He asked Dog to open his mouth wide so that he could pour the medicine down Dog's throat. The trusting friend did as he was told. He did not see the cunning look on Hare's face.

Then Hare pulled out four long thorns of an Umnga tree. He scratched Dog's throat so hard that Dog felt the most unbelievable pain. He cried out loud, 'Awoooo! Awoooo! What have you done to my voice? Now it's rough! You have made my voice rough, rough, rough!'

Dog jumped up and chased Hare. He was barking and barking from the

pain and the anger he was feeling. He chased after Hare but the trickster was long gone. What Hare had seen in Dog's eyes was worse than any danger he had ever faced before. He knew right away that if he caught him, Dog would kill him.

That beautiful night with a full moon saw the end of their friendship. And Dog never recovered his sweet singing voice. Up to this day, all he is left with is a rough, harsh bark and he chases every hare that crosses his path.

'Rough-rough! Rough-rough!'

Cosi, cosi, iyaphela

HERE I REST MY STORY

JOJELA'S WOODEN SPOON

Illustrations by Lungelo Gumede

JOJELA HAD BEEN MARRIED to Mamiya for years. They had lived in the same village as children and everyone knew them well. They always felt that they belonged together. So when they fell in love and got married, the whole village celebrated with them.

They were very happy together. The only problem was that Mamiya missed her husband when he was away – and he *loved* travelling.

Jojela went to nearby villages visiting their marketplaces. He took some of the things he had made with his own hands and sold them there. He made armbands, spears, bows and axes and made a good business selling them. Sometimes, if he liked a place, he stayed longer, meeting people and learning new skills. Then he returned to his wife and was thrilled to find her keeping their home warm and full of love. They talked for long hours and Jojela told her all about the people he had met and the places he had been to.

Then the next day he would go to visit friends, who were also happy to see him again. They welcomed him with home-brewed beer and meat as they sat down by the cattle kraal talking. They asked him many questions and they were so curious about all his travels in those unknown places. *This* was what Jojela loved to do.

Jojela always brought presents for his wife. She excitedly waited for the moment when he would take out something special from his travelling bag and hand it over to her. It could be a necklace, unusual bracelets or a beautifully woven cloth.

But one time Jojela came back with something for *himself*. It was a very beautifully carved wooden spoon. He proudly showed it to his wife and then told her that it was his and his alone. She was *not* allowed to eat with it.

Mamiya was shocked. She could not understand why this particular present had to be like this. She tried hard to hide how hurt she felt as she watched her husband eat with the spoon. She saw how much he seemed to enjoy the meal she gave him. Was it because of the spoon that his food was so much tastier than hers was? He did not want her to wash it either – he washed that spoon himself, with great care. Then he stood up and put it up on the thatch of the roof in their kitchen.

'Ne-ne-ne! Jojela, Jojela! What is happening to you?' his wife wondered to herself. Mamiya sat alone and thought hard. She wanted to feel what it was like to touch that special wooden spoon. She wanted to hold it in her hand – yes, and to eat with it. That would be great! But would that upset her husband very much? This was so difficult.

Two, three days went past and then she woke up one morning and said to herself: 'Today is the day! I am going try that wooden spoon! Yes! He! Ha!'

Jojela had his breakfast and went to visit a friend. Mamiya smiled and promised to cook him his favourite meal. As soon as she saw him disappear over the hill, she got to work. She took a wooden stool and climbed on it to try to reach the spoon.

Mamiya was quite short and she had to stand on her tiptoes and stretch her fingers to the roof. But no matter how she tried, it was just out of reach. And then, before she knew what was happening, she had lost her balance and came tumbling down. Some of the ashes on the fireplace were still hot and she was burned on her arms. Mamiya knew she had to clean up everything and make sure her husband did not suspect what she had been doing.

Later that afternoon Jojela came home and found his favourite meal ready for him. He pulled down his wooden spoon and sat down to enjoy his meal. And then he noticed that his wife had some burns on her arms.

'What happened to you?' he asked with concern.

'Um . . . um . . . I was cleaning the . . . the . . . kitchen and then I suddenly felt dizzy . . . and fell down,' she told him. He was sorry for her and gave her some aloe to soothe her pain.

When he had finished eating, he washed his beautifully carved spoon and put it back in the thatch grass inside the kitchen.

But Mamiya did not give up easily. She tried again. She planned everything carefully. As soon as her husband was gone she jumped up and got onto the wooden stool. Again she fell and this time sprained her ankle. Haai! This was more difficult than she had thought it would be!

Something was very wrong here. Why was Jojela so worried about her even touching his spoon? Was this a magical spoon? Still, one thing was clear in her mind. She would *not* give up. She would get hold of that spoon and eat with it too, no matter how difficult it was.

Next time she tried to touch the spoon, she first swept the fireplace. Then she put down a grass mat and a soft skin on it. On top of that she put a big flat rock. Last came the stool she had used before. She looked carefully at the spoon up on the thatch grass and knew exactly how she was going to get it. She stood comfortably on top of the stool and then reached up to the spoon easily. She held it in her hand, climbed down carefully and finally stood safely on the floor. How wonderful it felt. At last she had done it. She made a meal for herself, sat down and ate with that magical wooden spoon!

The first mouthful was just too delicious for words. She could not imagine why Jojela had not brought *two* of these magical spoons that added taste to any meal. She took the next mouthful, chewed slowly and swallowed. What

a good feeling it was to have tried again and again, and now she had succeeded. With a satisfied smile she put the spoon into her mouth.

And then, the spoon started moving *all by itself*. It was alive! It moved into her throat and got stuck. She had to swallow that food quickly and try to keep on breathing. The poor woman now got really scared. How was she going to call for help?

Mamiya crawled outside and sat in front of the kitchen sweating and waving her arms to get attention. She needed help *urgently*!

There was nobody at her neighbours' house and the other house was too far away for anybody to hear her.

Then her pig came and looked at her, sniffed about and grunted as it walked away. 'Gaw-gaw! Gaw-gaw!'

Then her goats came to her, hoping for something to eat. She tried to show them the spoon and to point at the path leading to where her husband was. 'Bbeheh-e, bheheh-e!' said the goats, and walked away.

The dog thought she was playing. It jumped about a bit, wagging its tail, but soon realised that she was making funny signs he did not understand. He too walked away, with his tongue hanging out.

Mamiya was terrified. What was going to happen to her? Just then the cock flapped his wings and called: 'Ah-kiki-li-kiii-ki!'

When he was done crowing he saw her, looked at the signs she was making, looked in the direction she was pointing and he understood.

The cock ran clumsily out of the gate and down the path to the first house over the little hill. There were men sitting by the cattle kraal, drinking and chatting happily. The cock climbed onto the stone wall and began to sing:

Kwathiwa ngizobika . . . Ah-ke-ke!
Umka Jojela . . . Ah-ke-ke!
Wemiwe yinenema . . . Ke-ke!
Isemphinjeni . . . Ke-ke!

I was sent to report . . . Ah-ke-ke!
That Jojela's wife . . . Ah-ke-ke!
Is hurt by a spoon . . . Ke-ke!
Stuck in her throat . . . Ke-ke!

The other men were irritated by this noise and they shouted for the cock to get away! But when he sang the song for the second time Jojela heard exactly what the cock was saying and he ran out of that place. Up the path leading to his house he ran. The cock followed him. Jojela found his wife sitting on the dirt outside their house. She was in great pain. He knelt down in front of her and gently moved the spoon *this* way and *that* way in an effort to pull it out. It was a slow process but he had to be careful. He did not want to hurt her any more. Tired and in great pain Mamiya looked up at the sky with tears running down her cheeks. She did not know how long it would take before that spoon was out of her throat. And when it did come out what would she say to her husband?

Finally Jojela managed to get the spoon out. He was so relieved! He gave his wife a broad smile. Then he took the spoon and right there and then, he broke it on his knee.

'I do not want this spoon if it will cause you so much pain. I want to see that beautiful smile of yours every day of my life, not tears like this,' he said, helping her to stand up. Together they went back into the house. But no matter what he said or how many times Jojela tried to get his wife to talk to him, she just looked at him with sad eyes and did not say a word.

This went on for days; Mamiya seemed to have lost her power of speech. Instead, she made signs for him whenever she was trying to tell him something.

After some time Jojela had to accept that Mamiya could not speak any more. But she started doing something new. She went collecting wood from the nearby forest. She began carving something that turned out to be a wooden spoon. Slowly and with great care she worked all day. When it was finished Jojela saw that it looked exactly like the spoon he had brought home – the spoon that caused his wife so much pain and took away her lovely voice. It looked so very beautiful when she finished it and she presented it to him with a loving smile – the first since the day he had come home with that wooden spoon. Jojela accepted Mamiya's spoon but did not use it.

Mamiya kept on working, making spoon after spoon. Each one was exactly like the first one. She worked like this every day and soon made other utensils, wooden meat trays and bowls.

Jojela had no desire to go out visiting any more. He wanted to stay at home and work. Together they carved and shaped many works of art. People came to buy from them. It looked like a small new market was starting. Some of their neighbours came to the house so they could all work together.

This was good indeed, but the best day in Jojela's life was when his wife made a delicious meal for all their friends. She served everyone and then gave each and every one of them a wooden spoon that she had carved with her own hands.

And then . . . slowly . . . Mamiya turned towards Jojela's friends and spoke. 'I love good food and good friends. And I love this man of mine. Thank you for sharing these special new times in our lives with us.' It was the first time she had spoken in months. The friends could hardly believe their ears. They had almost forgotten what her voice sounded like. Jojela looked at her and felt his heart swell with pride and the deepest love for his wife.

That wooden spoon changed their lives. So that is why, almost everywhere you travel in Africa, in every town and every village and every market, you will find beautiful carved wooden spoons.

Cosi, cosi, iyaphela

HERE I REST MY STORY

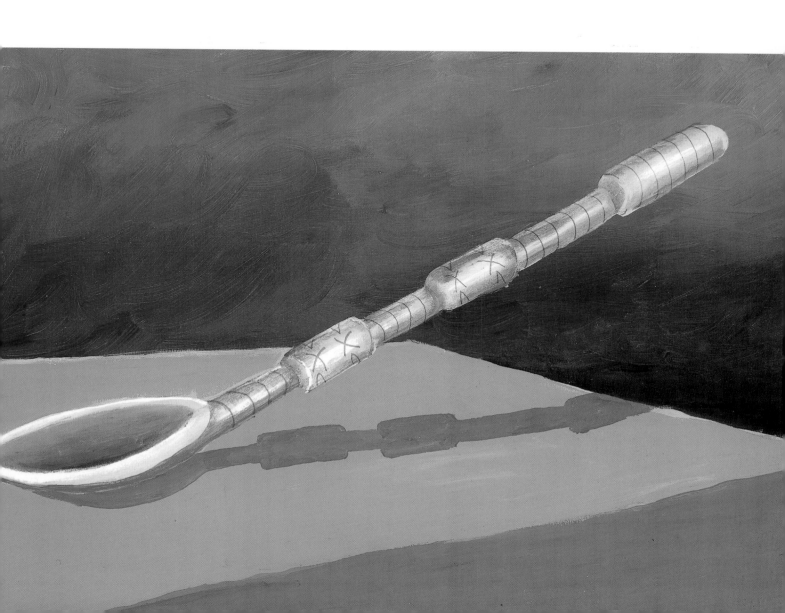

SUNSET COLOURS

Illustrations by Jeannie Kinsler

THEMBA WAS AN only child. He lived with his mother and father in a seaside village called Moyeni. He always dreamt that he would grow up one day and be a strong hunter like many big boys and men in his village. The men of Moyeni were known to be really good hunters and this is what many young boys wanted to do when they grew up. The chief and people of Moyeni were a proud people indeed.

Themba grew up always noticing the beauty surrounding him – the rolling hills, the majestic and thunderous ocean, the trees, flowers, colourful birds and all the other beauties of his home land. He liked drawing a lot and quickly he learned to use different flowers and herbs to make lovely colours to use. He had such a good eye for colours and a real talent for drawing beautiful pictures that were admired by many – young and old.

But no matter how good he got at drawing, no matter how many times he heard people praise him about what he did at such an early age, what he really, really wanted with all his heart was to be a great hunter. Themba expected that it was just a matter of one year – or maybe two – before the leader of the hunting team would call on his father to discuss his first hunting trip. Every time he thought about that wonderful day he got so excited. He could just see himself out in the big forests on a great hunt. What a happy day that would be!

Well, the years did pass and Themba grew older, but he was still very short – way too short for his sixteen years. Each time he asked his father or his older cousins when he would be called to join the hunting team, they told him that he was not cut out to be a hunter. The other boys laughed at him.

'You mean you cannot see that you are too short? What kind of little hunter will you make? Just continue with your funny drawings!'

Themba kept quiet. Sadly he had to wait for yet another year.

Maybe then he would have grown a little taller and bigger. *Then* he could join the proud Moyeni hunting team. The next year came and passed, and Themba remained short – shorter than his thirteen-year-old neighbours. This upset him a lot; he did not know what to do.

He started going up to the hill near his home almost every afternoon. He sat there alone looking at the countryside, admiring the beauty and wondering where the hunters were that day. Whatever he did, his mind travelled with the hunters. He could imagine all the places they went to. In his dreams he was always one of the bravest hunters.

One day Themba did not feel like drawing. He was sitting quietly at the top of the hill, watching and listening to the thunderous voice of the sea. He was trying to accept in his heart that maybe making pictures of great hunts was as far as he was going to get to being a hunter. His heart still ached a little.

Then he was suddenly aware of a very spectacular sunset. The colours were unbelievably beautiful; he just sat there, mesmerised by the magic of it all.

He was still staring when he saw a big cloud coming towards him. Sitting on the cloud was a very old man and a beautiful girl. Themba had not recovered from his shock when the cloud came even lower and closer. This was so scary! His heart was beating fast. 'What now?' he wondered. The old man on the cloud smiled at Themba.

'Do not be afraid of the special gift you have. It is good to be different!' he said softly. Then he reached down from his cloud and gave Themba an animal skin, soft and clean, all stretched out on four wooden poles. 'Please paint the colours of the sunset,' he asked Themba.

The beautiful girl smiled at Themba as if she knew him well. Then she began to sing:

Themba. Wena Themba,
Unesiphwo. Sisibenzise.
Ulithemba lesizwe sakho.

Themba, you have a gift. Use it.
You are the hope of your people.

The old man and the beautiful girl waved goodbye as the big cloud carried them away.

* * *

It was dark by the time Themba got home. For days after that he struggled to recapture the colours of the magical sunset he had seen that evening, but he couldn't. He told everyone to leave him alone. Everything he painted came out wishy-washy and grey. He could not capture the magical moments when the old man spoke to him and the beautiful girl sang. He wanted to make for himself that wonderful burst of colours. He practised a few times on tree bark. But although he had it in his mind, he could not put it down. He watched many sunsets but none was as special. Themba was becoming sadder by the day.

One day Themba sat again at his place on the hill. The sky was dark and grey – like dirty dishwater. He could feel the tears pricking his eyes. 'I am not good for anything,' he thought to himself. 'I am not a member of our proud hunting team, and now I have failed to do something I thought I was really good at. I don't want to live any more!'

Could it be that those lovely people had come to the wrong village? Had found the wrong Themba? But he did not really want to believe that. 'I *am* the right Themba!' he told himself fiercely.

With his eyes closed tight, he wished for a sunset as beautiful as the one he had seen so many weeks ago when the mysterious old man came and asked him to paint the difficult drawing. He waited there for some time with his animal skin, wishing for one last try.

When the sunset colours slowly collected, he thought he was dreaming. The magical sunset was upon him again! Oh, no! He had not brought any of his paint sticks to draw with. Why was this happening to him? Then he saw the cloud coming towards him again. This time the girl was alone. In a calabash she carried many paint sticks, each one thick with paint in a lovely colour.

'This is my gift to you,' she said. 'Don't be so sad, because *you* are a gift to your people.' And then she began to sing. As she sang, Themba's heart filled with happiness.

Themba. Wena Themba,
Unesiphwo. Sisibenzise.
Ulithemba lesizwe sakho.

Themba, you have a gift. Use it.
You are the hope of your people.

Themba accepted her gift and started to work, very fast and with great excitement. Each time he used a fresh paint stick on his soft animal skin, he shouted 'Thank you!' to the beautiful girl who was smiling brightly as the cloud carried her away.

He worked fast, not wanting to lose any of the sunset colours. When he was finished, there was hardly any light left. He ran down the hill to show his parents and tell them everything that had happened. The next day the chief and the village elders saw his wonderful work. They told him they were very proud of him. The chief said that he had one request, 'Make a portrait of me.'

This Themba did with great joy, and the next week he was busy with the portrait of another elder . . . and another . . . and another. He was so busy that he had no time for regrets.

As the elders remembered their stories, they called to Themba to come and listen and he painted their memories. When the hunters returned from a hunt, they looked for Themba to draw their stories. Sometimes the stories made Themba sad – but other times he laughed as he painted.

Now many people admired Themba. Some of them even wished they could learn to draw too. He never grew to be tall or big physically, but his work made him very big and tall in the eyes of all who met him.

The colours of the sunset gave back Themba's wish to live. The sunset magic gave him self-respect.

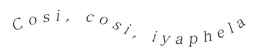

Cosi, cosi, iyaphela

HERE I REST MY STORY

ABOUT THE ARTISTS

 KALLE BECKER was born in Göettingen, Germany, in 1964. He studied graphics, filmmaking, photography and Russian in both Germany and the Ukraine. As a filmmaker and actor, he has worked in Germany, Russia, Georgia and South Africa. He is also a freelance artist and illustrated Gcina Mhlophe's storybooks *Fudukazi's Magic* and *Stories of Africa*. Now based in Durban, Kalle is married to Gcina Mhlophe and they have one daughter. For more about Kalle, go to www.kallebecker.com.

 LUNGELO GUMEDE did his first formal art training at the Bat Centre Studio in Durban in 2003. He has since studied Fine Art at the Durban Institute of Technology and is enrolled at Unisa as a Visual Arts student. Lungelo works from the Bat Centre where he facilitates Saturday art classes and workshops, and does portrait and wildlife paintings, as well as sculptures and busts on commission. His work has been exhibited in New York, Réunion and Turkey. For more about Lungelo, go to www.african-artist.co.za.

 JEANNIE KINSLER trained and worked as a graphic designer for many years before she started to paint full time in 1998. She now works from home as an artist and illustrator and her favourite medium is oil painting. She has illustrated four of Gcina Mhlophe's books, including *Stories of Africa*. Jeannie lives in Durban with her husband and three daughters.

 SUSET MAAKAL is an Associate of the South African Watercolour Society. Some of her work forms part of the permanent collection of the KwaZulu-Natal Museum Services and she has also completed commissions for corporate art works. Suset teaches watercolour painting to both adults and children. She lives in Newcastle and is married with four children and four grandchildren. Suset's gallery is part of the Open Studio Route in Northern KwaZulu-Natal, and she can be emailed on Suset@lantic.net.

 LALELANI MBHELE is a KwaMashu-based artist whose formal art training began only after he left school. In 1997, he participated in a one-year workshop programme at the African Art Centre, and then went on to study at Natal Technikon for his Fine Art Diploma, which he hopes to complete soon. Lalelani is currently one of the resident artists at the Bat Centre Studio in Durban. He was one of the illustrators in Gcina Mhlophe's *Stories of Africa* and his favourite mediums are woodcut and watercolour.